SCREAM STREET

FANG OF THE VAMPIRE

"Lightning-paced, bloodcurdling fun. I wish
I'd been able to visit Scream Street as a kid!"
Darren Shan

The fiendish fun continues at
www.screamstreet.co.uk

Other Scream Street titles:

Blood of the Witch

Heart of the Mummy

Flesh of the Zombie

Coming soon:

Skull of the Skeleton

Claw of the Werewolf

SCREAM STREET

FANG OF THE VAMPIRE

TOMMY DNBAVAND

**WALKER
BOOKS**

First published 2008 by Walker Books Ltd
87 Vauxhall Walk, London SE11 5HJ

2 4 6 8 10 9 7 5 3 1

Text © 2008 Tommy Donbavand
Illustrations © 2008 Cartoon Saloon Ltd

This book has been typeset in Bembo Educational

Printed and bound in Great Britain by Clays Ltd, St Ives plc

British Library Cataloguing in Publication Data: a catalogue record
for this book is available from the British Library

ISBN 978-1-4063-1424-3 (trade edition)
ISBN 978-1-4063-2060-2 (library edition)

www.walker.co.uk

For Mum: here are the keys to
the biggest house on Scream Street

Meet the residents...

Luke Watson

Cleo Farr

Resus Negative

Dixon

Sir Otto Sneer

Samuel Skipstone

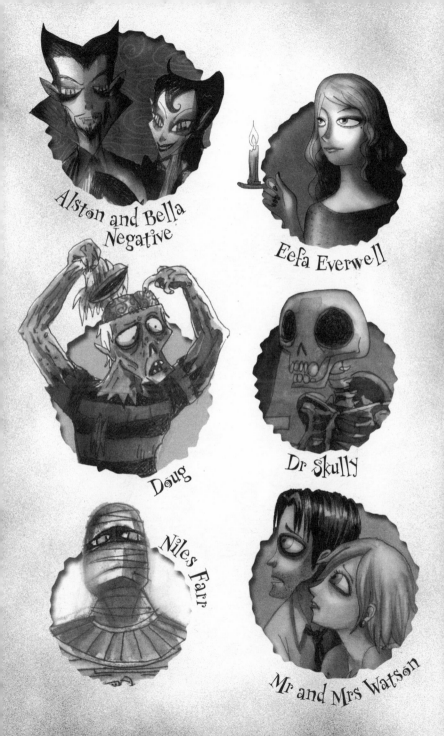

Alston and Bella Negative

Eefa Everwell

Doug

Dr Skully

Niles Farr

Mr and Mrs Watson

Welcome to Scream Street

Who lives where...

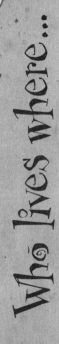

Chapter One
The Chase

The schoolboy leapt over the wall into the graveyard, his feet skidding on wet grass. Barely managing to keep his balance he ran on, dodging between headstones that jutted from the ground like rotten teeth.

Behind him the creature landed in the mud, still transforming. It roared as its razor-sharp claws ripped through the black leather of its shoes and glinted in the weak sunlight. Tearing away what remained of its footwear with yellowing nails, the monster gave chase.

The boy tripped and fell, banging his head on a gravestone. A flash of white filled his vision and he was temporarily stunned. Forcing himself to stand, the schoolboy rubbed at the cut on his forehead. Staring at the red liquid smeared across his finger-tips, he heard a snarl.

The creature was in front of him now, approaching, its eyes never leaving his own. The boy was reminded of nature programmes on TV in which lions stalked their prey. He stepped back and found himself pressed against the cold marble of an ornate headstone. He was trapped.

The creature screamed as its face began to push outwards, bones splintering noisily and quickly reforming; muscles tearing, then instantly knotting together as its entire head changed shape. Strands of thick fur pushed out of every pore of its skin.

The fully formed werewolf lifted its snout to the sky and howled.

"N-no!" stuttered the schoolboy. "Please don't hurt me!" He tried to run, but the werewolf was on him in a second, lashing out with its claws.

Four crimson lines soaked into the material of the boy's torn white school shirt as he fell to the ground once again. He pushed himself backwards across the muddy grass as the monster sniffed at the air, the scent of blood filling its nostrils. Baring its teeth, the wolf prepared to leap for its victim.

Suddenly a yapping sound distracted the creature, and it spun to see a small chihuahua

bounding around its legs and nipping at its back paws. In the distance a voice could be heard to call out, "Fluffy! Here, boy!"

The monster kicked the yelping dog away and turned back to its prey. As the schoolboy screamed, the chihuahua bit the werewolf hard on the leg and disappeared into the bushes.

Roaring with rage, the wolf turned and raced after the dog.

Chapter Two
The Move

Luke Watson turned the dog collar over in his hands, wiping dried blood from the name tag to reveal the word FLUFFY. The chihuahua had wriggled out of its collar and run away as the werewolf caught hold of it, a cut on the

ear the only evidence that it had been in a fight at all.

Hearing a sound on the stairs, Luke stuffed the collar under his pillow and grabbed the game-pad of his computer console, resuming his battle against the evil mechanoids. "Come in," he called in response to a quiet tap on his bedroom door.

His mum entered, carrying a tray of food. Luke glanced at the meal: vegetarian again. His parents hadn't cooked him meat for almost a year now.

"Got onto the next level yet?" his mum asked, putting the tray down on the desk.

Luke shook his head. "I've got rid of the robot generals, but I need to kill the overlord before I can progress to the mother ship."

Mrs Watson sat down on the bed. She said nothing for a while, then softly cleared her throat. "I spoke to Steven Black's parents."

"I thought Dad was going to ring them."

"He's not back from work yet," explained his mum.

Luke tried unsuccessfully to hide the irritation in his voice. "Figures!"

"Steven told his parents he hurt his chest

 16

climbing over a barbed

Luke concentrated on t

"Why him, Luke? You've g
friends at school as it is."

"He's no friend!" snapped Luke, thro
gamepad onto the bed. "He's a bully! He ni
some girl's bag on the way home from school;
I was just trying to get it back for her. There was
no reason for him to turn on me!"

"He didn't know what would happen," said
his mum. "He didn't know that you would…"
She sighed, leaving the sentence unfinished. "The
scratches aren't deep," she said. "It's going to be
OK. This time."

Luke studied his mum as she picked up the
gamepad and did her best to fight a battalion of
robots wielding laser pistols. Neither of his parents had smiled for a long time. Not since he had
first transformed into a werewolf.

"You know," he said with a grin, "you suck
at this game!" Mrs Watson punched him playfully on the arm as he snatched the controls from
her. "You only ever press one button at a time.
But if you press a combination—"

A smash came from downstairs.

wire fence," said his mum.
e game, silent.
got few enough
wing the
ked

t a time and
hall were full
mily's belong-
ture out of the
purple jumpsuit
the back.

ng up the remains
d, just home from
he pieces away from

him. The man ... a hand and pressed it over Mr Watson's eyes. Luke watched in terror as his dad crumpled to the floor.

"Mike!" yelled Luke's mum, rushing in. She dropped to her knees beside her husband and grabbed his wrist, checking for a pulse. The blond man laid his palm over her face and she too collapsed, with a moan.

Luke raced across the room, fighting to get to his parents. One of the men gripped his arm and pulled him back so that two of his colleagues could pass by with a large picture. They stepped over Mr and Mrs Watson as if they were nothing more than lumps in the carpet.

Luke grabbed the shoulder of the man whose

touch had knocked out his parents, spinning him round. "What have you…" The words stuck in his throat.

The man's head had no features – no eyes, nose, ears or mouth. Just a smooth layer of skin. Luke glanced around the room. All the men were the same.

"Who are you?" he demanded, backing away. He fell onto the sofa, kicking out as the man

pressed three fingertips to the side of his head. Luke suddenly became aware of a voice flooding his mind.

"We are the Movers," said the voice. "You are being moved."

Luke stared up into the featureless face. "Why?"

"You attacked a boy."

"But he got away when I…" Luke stumbled over his words. "When the wolf chased the chihuahua! He won't tell anyone about me, honest!"

The explanation made no difference. The Mover pulled his hand away and turned to pick up a framed photograph. Luke jumped to his feet and dashed after the man, stopping as he noticed that his parents had gone.

"Where are they?" he shouted. "What have you done with my parents?"

The sound of a zip being closed caught his attention and Luke dashed to the kitchen to discover another Mover sealing his mum inside a purple bag. An identical bag, presumably containing his dad, lay on the table.

"Let them go!" he screamed, launching himself

at the faceless man and trying to unzip the bag. Luke didn't see the second Mover until his hand covered Luke's face and the world dissolved into a fizzing pool of purple light.

Luke woke up in near darkness. He was lying on his bed, a dull pain throbbing behind his eyes. Groaning, he reached for the glass of water on his bedside table. A few gulps cleared his dry throat, and he sat upright.

Luke froze. He was on his bed, but this wasn't his room. A large glass chandelier hung from the high ceiling above him. The walls were painted green and the floor was a deep, polished wood. A purple bag, smaller than the one in which he had seen his parents wrapped, lay over the end of the bed.

The tray of dinner sat beside his homework on the desk and the games console was in its place on top of the now dark computer monitor. Luke leant over and pressed the ON switch but the screen didn't seem to be working. Sliding his hand beneath his pillow, he pulled out the blood-soaked dog collar. All his stuff was here; this just wasn't his bedroom.

Luke swung his legs off the bed, stuffing the

21

dog collar into his pocket. He found his trainers and slid them on, then went over to the bookshelf and ran his fingers over his books to check they were all real. They were.

Opening the heavy door, Luke found himself standing at the top of an ornately carved stairway. A thick black rug at his feet appeared to be moving, and it was a moment before Luke realized he was looking at hundreds of spiders. They crawled across the landing as one, dragging tiny webbing sacks of dust and leaving behind a trail of clean, red carpet. The spiders were vacuuming.

Luke crossed the landing and checked inside the other rooms on the top floor of the house. His parents' bedroom was as it should be, their wrought-iron bedstead and wardrobes all in place. Two purple body bags lay, discarded, on the bedroom floor.

The bathroom was basic, with a bare stone floor and an ancient bathtub. Gas lamps hung from the walls. Luke reached out to test one when he heard muffled voices.

Heading downstairs, he found a living room lined with dark wood panelling; the family's brightly coloured sofa looked out of place in such

22

ornate surroundings. Spiders were at work here, too, cleaning the deep-pile carpet.

Hearing the voices again, Luke went back out into the hallway. He pushed open a door on his right to reveal an old kitchen. His parents sat together at one end of a long wooden table.

"Mum!" yelled Luke as he ran across the kitchen and flung his arms around her. She was shaking. "Where are we?"

"We don't know," said Luke's dad. "We came round to find ourselves on our bed in some room upstairs. We found you but couldn't wake you up."

"And we're wearing these," added Mrs Watson, holding up her arm to reveal a bracelet, like those used for hospital patients, stamped with the number 13. Luke checked his own wrist and discovered an identical band.

Someone hammered at the front door.

"Stay here," said Luke, tearing the strip of paper from his wrist and dashing back out into the hallway.

"Luke, no!" His mum grabbed for his arm, but he was already leaving the room.

Three figures were silhouetted against the

frosted glass of the front door. Luke approached cautiously, sliding back the solid brass bolts and opening the door just enough to peer out into the cold air.

"Welcome to Scream Street!" boomed a voice. Luke swallowed hard. Standing on the doorstep was a family of vampires.

Chapter Three
The Attack

The tallest vampire
threw his cape aside,
grabbed Luke's hand
and shook it furiously.
"Alston Negative's the
name. This is my wife,
Bella, and our son,
Resus!"

"We're your new neighbours," said the woman, striding past Luke towards the kitchen doorway. Mr and Mrs Watson stood there, mouths open.

"No!" Luke shouted, struggling to free himself from the handshake. Before he could move, the female vampire had reached beneath her cape and produced a vase of dead roses, handing the gift to Luke's mum. Thick red liquid filled the container. It was blood.

Mrs Watson paled. Luke ran, catching her just as she began to faint. The vase smashed to the floor, spraying blood up the walls. The younger vampire darted past his father and helped Luke to sit his mum on the stairs, wafting his cape in front of her face.

Luke studied the boy. He looked about the same age as himself, although he had jet-black hair and white skin with dark rings around his eyes. Sharp fangs protruded from the boy's mouth.

"Are you a real vampire?" Luke asked.

Resus stared at him. "What do you think?"

"Why don't you two boys head upstairs and play?" said Bella, stepping in to take charge of

Mrs Watson. "We'll clean up and make sure your mum is all right."

"I think I should stay," said Luke, squeezing his mum's hand as she came round from her faint.

"It's OK," said Mr Watson. "I think we need to find out what's going on."

"If you're sure…" said Luke, checking for the slightest indication that his parents wanted him to remain with them. Mr Watson nodded, and Luke reluctantly led Resus Negative up to his room.

Resus grabbed a gory horror novel from the bookshelf and flopped onto the bed to read. Luke closed the door and watched the young vampire for a moment. "So, are you going to bite my neck and suck my blood?"

Resus didn't look up. "Not unless you annoy me."

Luke took a deep breath. What type of conversation did you have with a vampire? "Have you read that one before?" he asked, gesturing towards the book.

"We're not backward here, you know," said Resus, turning the page.

"I didn't mean that. I just thought…"

There was an awkward silence. Luke noticed black droplets trickling down the vampire's neck. "Your hair dye is running."

Resus spun round, pulling his cape up higher around his neck. "It's not dye!" he snapped. "My hair is naturally this colour! All vampires have black hair."

"I was just saying," replied Luke. "Check it in the mirror if you like."

"I can't," growled Resus. "I'm a vampire. I don't have a reflection."

"But I can see your reflection," said Luke, pointing to the mirror above his desk.

Resus slammed the book closed. "Look, I'm not happy about being sent up here either," he said, "but my dad asked me to be pleasant to you." He opened the book again as if to continue reading. "I thought you were going to be another vampire or, at the very least, a troll. But you're just a normal. G.H.O.U.L. had no business bringing you here."

"G.H.O.U.L.!" gasped Luke. "That was written on the backs of the faceless men. What does it mean?"

 28

"Government Housing Of Unusual Life-forms," muttered Resus. "And by 'faceless men' I presume you mean the Movers?"

"You've seen them?" asked Luke.

"They're everywhere when we have a new family move in," said Resus. "Although I think they went to the wrong address this time."

Luke sighed. Unusual life-forms. Is that what people thought of him now? "What's a normal?" he asked.

Resus turned another page. "You don't know anything, do you. *You're* a normal! Someone from the outside. Someone who doesn't belong here."

Luke turned to gaze out of the window. Resus pulled a can of black hairspray from inside his cloak and gave his fringe a quick blast.

"I'm a werewolf," said Luke.

Resus stuffed the can back inside his cape. "For real?"

"I first transformed a year ago, on my birthday," explained Luke. "My parents thought I was having some sort of fit until the claws appeared."

"Do I have to be wary of you when there's a full moon?" asked the vampire.

Luke shook his head. "That's just in films. I change whenever I get angry."

"And that's what happened the first time?"

"My dad missed my party because he was working late," said Luke. "When he came home I remember shouting at him, then nothing else. Next thing I know, I'm strapped to a hospital bed being injected with everything the doctors can find." Luke stared at the ghostly reflection of himself in the window. "That's when they told me I'd attacked my dad."

"Did you hurt him?" asked Resus.

"It would have been worse, but my parents managed to tie me up. If they hadn't, I don't know what I—"

A book bounced off the back of Luke's head and he spun round angrily. "What was that for?" he shouted.

"That wasn't me!" said Resus. "It just flew across the room!"

"Yeah, right," said Luke. "A book jumped off the desk by itself and hit me."

"It's true!" said Resus. As he spoke, Luke's desk lamp rose into the air. The vampire ducked as the lamp smashed against the wall behind him.

Within seconds, everything was moving: books, CDs, games – each item taking flight. Luke raced for the door. "What's happening?"

"It's a poltergeist attack!" said Resus as the tray of cold food hit him full in the face. "Lentil bake?" he asked scornfully.

Luke dodged a thick science textbook. "I'd kill for a beefburger!"

The boys dashed downstairs to discover the two older vampires in the kitchen, doing their best to protect Luke's parents from soaring items of furniture.

"Dad! What can we do?" yelled Resus, jumping as a chair whizzed past.

"Go to Everwell's!" shouted Alston. "See if Eefa has finished that spell yet."

Nodding, Resus ran for the open front door and disappeared into the darkness beyond. With a glance back at his mum and dad, Luke followed.

Outside, Luke got his first look at Scream Street. Number 13, his new home, was tall and mis-shapen, towering high into the air. Its black slate roof appeared to almost pierce the thick grey clouds lurking above.

Gas lamps flickered on the tops of iron posts, casting spindly shadows of the dead trees that punctuated the pavement. A cold wind howled, banging gates and slamming window shutters.

"What's Everwell's?" asked Luke, catching up with Resus.

"Everwell's Emporium," explained the vampire. "Eefa Everwell is a witch. She's been working on a spell to stop the poltergeist attacks."

"Polter*what* attacks?" asked Luke, pulling Resus into a hedge as a metal dustbin shot along the pavement towards them.

"Polter*geist*!" shouted Resus as the dustbin clattered past. "A type of ghost that can move things. They're known to have a bit of a temper!"

The vampire climbed out of the bush and ran on. Luke began to follow, when a hand burst out of the soil and grabbed his ankle. A head appeared beside the hand: a head with green cracked skin, broken teeth and dull eyes. Luke had played enough computer games to know what had hold of his leg.

It was a zombie.

Chapter Four
The Transformation

"**Resus!**" yelled Luke. His voice was swallowed up by the howling wind and the vampire continued running, unaware that he was now alone.

Luke turned back to try to free his leg. The hand that gripped it was covered in scabs and sores. Broken fingernails were blackened with

dirt and dried blood. If he tried to pull free, he was likely to be scratched and possibly infected with some terrible disease.

Luke gazed into the zombie's milky eyes. The creature grinned at him, revealing a mouth crawling with lice and maggots. A cockroach scuttled out of a nostril and up into the zombie's left ear, dragging a trail of black snot behind it.

"Dude!" the zombie said. "What's the scoop?"

Luke stared at the hideous creature. Had it really spoken to him? Surely zombies were more interested in consuming your brains than engaging you in conversation?

"Excuse me?"

"Everything's, like, whizzing around, man!" continued the monster. "Caught me off guard and I totally lost my leg!"

"It's, er, a poltergeist attack," explained Luke. "They're known to have a bit of a temper, apparently."

"Poltergeist..." mused the zombie aloud. "Bogus, dude!"

"Absolutely!" agreed Luke, gesturing towards the creature's grip on his ankle. "But I'm afraid this is *my* leg, not yours."

"No way!"

"Yes," said Luke. "Sorry."

Resus reappeared beside him. "I wondered where you'd got to."

"Busy meeting the locals," said Luke.

"What's the matter, Doug?" Resus asked.

"It's totally tripping me out, man!" replied the zombie. "The new dude here reckons this leg is his!"

"It is," said Resus. He peered through the hedge and spotted something wedged behind a garden gate. "I think you'll find *this* leg is yours," he added, retrieving the green-skinned limb.

"Far out, little vampire dude!" beamed Doug. The zombie released Luke's ankle and began to sink back into the ground. "Turf!" he yelled as the hole closed in over his greasy, matted hair. "I found it! Get the sewing kit, man!"

As Resus helped him to his feet, Luke made a mental note to be much kinder to computer-game zombies from now on.

The road widened into a square. Luke noticed there were other roads leading away from it: eight in total. Scream Street was shaped like a giant spider.

Standing proudly on one side of the square was a large shop: a brightly lit sign announced that this was Everwell's Emporium. Resus pushed open its silver doors and stepped inside. A bat tethered to a perch above the doorway let out a piercing squeal to announce the arrival of another customer.

Luke had barely followed him in when a shining sphere shot straight for his head, and he had to duck to avoid being hit. The fortune-

teller's crystal ball shattered into a thousand pieces against the door frame. The shop was in chaos: glass bottles and coloured gems soared around the ceiling as the poltergeist attack continued to grow in strength.

In the centre of the shop stood a small figure wrapped from head to toe in bandages. It gazed intently into a handheld mirror, ignoring the mayhem around it.

"Cleo?" said Resus. "What are you doing here?"

The girl shoved the mirror out of sight and rubbed furiously at a pink stain on the dressings around her mouth. "I, er, just came to see if Eefa had finished putting her spell together!"

Resus stared at her. "Are you wearing lipstick?" he asked.

"Don't be ridiculous," replied Cleo, pulling bandages up from her chin to conceal the colourful blemish.

"You're a mummy!" Luke exclaimed.

"Not yet," replied the girl. "I'm much too young to have children!"

"No, I meant—"

"Just messing with you!" The mummy punched

him playfully on the arm. "I'm Cleo," she said. "You must be the new kid." The trio jumped as a shelving unit crashed to the floor behind them. "What a welcome to Scream Street this is!"

"He's a werewolf," announced Resus.

Cleo's eyes widened. "What, with all the claws and howling and stuff?"

Luke nodded.

"Cool!"

"Where's Eefa?" asked Resus.

"In here!" shouted a voice. Eefa Everwell appeared from a doorway at the back of the shop, protecting herself from flying objects with a circular tray. Luke blinked. *This* was a witch? Instead of the wart-covered hag he had imagined, Eefa Everwell was stunningly beautiful.

Pure white hair streaked with silver ran down her back. Her flawless skin was complemented by her dark violet lipstick and nail polish. Eyes the colour of emeralds smiled at Luke.

Resus reached over and closed Luke's mouth. "Don't worry," he said, grinning. "Eefa has this effect on everyone. It's some kind of enchantment charm. You'll soon learn to ignore her."

Luke had just decided he wanted nothing

more than to stare at this vision of beauty for the rest of his life, when a lamp shaped like a dragon bounced off his head, jolting him back to reality. Cleo grabbed his hand and dragged him behind the counter. Resus and Eefa joined them.

"Have you finished the spell, Eefa?" asked Cleo.

"Almost," the witch said, gesturing towards a scroll of parchment whirling around the centre of the shop, "but it was pulled out of my hands when the attack started."

"I'll get it!" shouted Cleo. Before anyone could stop her, the mummy had climbed on top of the counter and jumped into the commotion beyond. A windchime crashed down from the ceiling and she was forced to swerve to one side.

"Get back here!" yelled Resus.

Cleo stuck her tongue out at him as she snatched the parchment from the air. "Got it!" she grinned. She was running back to the safety of the counter when a jar of pulsing blue liquid smashed into a display of scented candles. The liquid sprayed over the candle flames and a ball of fire exploded into the air.

Cleo was thrown back by the blast, smashing

into the wall and collapsing beneath a large cotton wall-hanging. The fire spread quickly. Luke leapt over the counter and pulled the burning wall-hanging off the mummy, but it was too late. Cleo was on fire.

The mummy screamed as her bandages burned. Eefa grabbed a rug and began beating at the flames. "Resus!" she shrieked. "Get some water!"

Luke glanced up at the vampire. Resus was rooted to the spot, licking the tips of his fangs as he studied the flames, the fire reflected in his dark eyes.

Turning back to the blaze, Luke spotted a gap in the flames and dashed forward. Clutching Cleo's hand, he began to drag her away from the inferno. With a roar, the flames exploded, throwing him to the floor.

Luke jumped back to his feet, angrily rubbing at his scorched flesh. His eyes opened wide as a familiar feeling washed over him. His head swam and everything slowed to a crawl inside his mind. He was starting to transform.

"Not now!" he pleaded aloud, but the change had already begun. Wolf fur spread across his body like a thick blanket and Luke gritted his teeth against the agony that was to come. To his amazement, nothing else happened. The transformation stopped after the fur was in place.

Luke discovered his skin was now shielded from the heat of the fire, and cautiously he stepped into the flames. His clothes quickly burnt away, but the dense fur protected his body. Lifting Cleo, Luke carried her out of the fire and laid her on the shop counter.

Eefa hurried to the mummy, raising her hands over her burnt body and chanting under her breath. Cleo cried softly with the pain.

Then there was a sound like wind being sucked down a drain, and the bottles and jars still flying through the air fell to the floor with a smash. The poltergeist attack was over as quickly as it had started.

Luke tore a curtain from the window and wrapped it around himself as the thick strands of fur retracted into his skin. Within seconds he was human again.

Resus crunched over to him through the broken glass. "That was amazing!" he said. "I just froze, but you were great. How did you do that?"

"I don't know," replied Luke. "I didn't change completely."

Eefa looked up from the spell she was working over Cleo. "You're in Scream Street," she said. "Werewolves have lived here before and they all experienced partial transformations of some kind or another."

Resus clapped Luke on the back. "I take back what I said earlier," he beamed. "You're anything but a normal."

Luke allowed himself a smile. Perhaps living in Scream Street wouldn't be so bad after all...

His thoughts were interrupted by the screech of the bat as the door opened. Bella Negative appeared, a serious expression on her face.

"Luke," she said. "It's your mum."

Chapter Five
The Landlord

Back in the kitchen of 13 Scream Street, Luke watched as Bella Negative bandaged his mum's broken arm.

"We were sheltering beneath the table when the iron stove flew over and hit your mum," said Alston. "There was nothing we could do."

"What about magic?" asked Luke. "Eefa was helping Cleo at the shop."

"Eefa was just easing Cleo's pain," said Bella.

"Injuries have to heal naturally here, just like in your world."

"*My* world!" snapped Luke. "None of this would have happened if we had just been left alone in 'my world'!"

"This is your world now," said Bella. "You're a werewolf; you belong here."

"My mum and dad don't belong here, though, do they?" shouted Luke. He spun round. "Look at them! They're terrified."

"Luke," said Mr Watson. "It's OK…"

"No, Dad, it's not OK," said Luke. "This is all my fault – you're here because of me! I'm taking you home."

"That's impossible," said Alston, "unless you're Samuel Skipstone."

"Who?"

"Samuel Skipstone wrote a book about Scream Street," explained Bella. "Legend says he discovered the only way out."

"Then I'll read that!" said Luke.

"It's nothing but a fairy tale," insisted Alston. "Once you've been brought to Scream Street, you're here to stay."

"That's ridiculous!" shouted Luke. "There

must be a way out. We can't—"

The front door smashed open and then a large, sweating man appeared in the kitchen doorway, puffing at a thick cigar. Foul smoke filled the air around him.

"Sir Otto!" said Alston.

"Why are all the lights on in this house?" roared the man, stroking a silk scarf that covered his neck. "You're wasting gas!"

"We've been clearing up after the poltergeist attack," explained Bella. "This family has just arrived and Mrs Watson has broken her arm."

The man opened his mouth to reply but stopped when a tall, thin figure with lank ginger hair entered the room. "I don't get it, Uncle Otto," he said.

"How many times do I have to tell you, Dixon?" the man growled. "When we're out in public, you are to refer to me as *Sir*."

"Sorry, Sir Uncle Otto," smiled Dixon. "I just don't understand why you got me to kick the door down when there are people inside. We could have knocked!"

Sir Otto slapped his nephew across the head. "Idiot!" Regaining his composure, he turned back to Bella. "You know the rules! Only one light to be burning at a time. No exceptions!"

Sir Otto pulled the cigar out of his mouth and smiled nastily at Luke. "Hello, little freak," he purred. "I'm Sir Otto Sneer, your new

 47

landlord." Then he turned to his nephew. "Dixon," he roared, jamming the cigar back between his lips. "Disconnect them!"

"You can't!" shouted Alston. "They need gas!"

"Then they should have obeyed the rules," snarled the landlord as he disappeared out into the street. Within minutes, the house was plunged into darkness. The only sound was of Mrs Watson sobbing.

"I've got to take my mum and dad home," muttered Luke.

Bella appeared beside him. "There might be a way," she whispered. "But you'll have to do some work first."

"What kind of work?" asked Luke.

"Schoolwork!"

"And, of course, a very warm welcome to our newest pupil!"

Luke stared at his new teacher – or, rather, *through* his new teacher. Dr Skully was a skeleton. "I spent a long career as a laboratory skeleton," he had explained earlier. "Now retired, I devote my life to teaching others."

Luke was sitting with Resus and Cleo in Dr Skully's dining room, set up as a classroom complete with desks, a blackboard and bookshelves.

"Biscuit, anyone?" asked the teacher's skeletal wife as she entered with a tray of hot drinks and snacks.

"Really, Tibia," scolded the teacher lightly. "How many times must I ask you not to simply barge in without— Oh, my, are those chocolate chip?"

Luke took the opportunity to lean across and whisper to Resus, "This is all very cosy, but how does it help me get my parents home?"

"My mum said there's a book that shows how to open a doorway to your world," replied the vampire. "*Skipstone's Tales of Scream Street.*"

"Skipstone?" said Cleo. "The man who claimed the Loch Ness Monster lived in his toilet bowl? Everyone knows his stories are crazy!"

Resus shrugged. "Even the weirdest nursery rhyme has some truth in it."

"OK," said Cleo, "it's worth a try. But how do we find the book?"

"What do you mean 'we'?" hissed Luke. "I'm doing this alone."

"No, you're not!" said Cleo. "I lay in silence for centuries while explorers searched my tomb. Now there's an adventure on my doorstep, I'm not missing it!"

"You can count me in too!" grinned Resus.

Luke was surprised to feel relieved. He had no idea what might be involved in opening this doorway, and any help he could get would be welcome.

"Right!" said Dr Skully as he munched on a cookie. The crumbs bounced off his ribcage as they fell to the floor. "Maths books open to chapter—"

"Could you tell us about Samuel Skipstone, please, sir?" interrupted Resus.

"Skipstone?" said the teacher. "School is a place for facts, Master Negative, not the exploration of fictitious ramblings!" The skeleton shook his head. "Today we are here to study mathematics."

Luke sighed as Dr Skully turned to the blackboard to write out a complicated algebra equation. "What do we do now?"

"Find the book ourselves," replied Resus. "If anyone's got a copy, it will be Dr Skully. We just need to search these bookcases."

"But how do we get him out of the room?" hissed Cleo.

Resus winked. "Leave it to me!" He reached inside his cloak and pulled out a large bone, rotting shreds of meat still attached.

"Where did you get that?" asked Luke.

"You can thank my grandad," replied Resus.

"He gave you that leg bone?" said Luke.

"This *is* his leg bone!" grinned the vampire.

"You're disgusting," moaned Cleo.

"Why?" said Resus. "He doesn't need it; he's been dead for years! Now, check this out…"

He waggled the bone beneath the desk. "Scapula, here, boy!"

A skeleton dog padded into the room and took the bone in its teeth. It trotted through the open back door and out to a hole in the garden. Suddenly the dog seemed to become confused, and after looking from the bone to its own skeletal body and back again, it jumped into the hole and covered itself with soil.

"Dr Skully," called Resus, "Scapula's burying himself in the garden again."

"Oh, dear!" groaned the teacher, running from the room.

Resus leapt to his feet. "Right, we've got about two minutes!" he said. "We're looking for *Skipstone's Tales of Scream Street*."

Luke began to search. The teacher's shelves featured titles such as *Dragon Wrangling*, *In Touch with the Spirits* and *101 Ways to Clean Up After a Bog Monster*, but there was no sign of *Skipstone's Tales of Scream Street*. "This is hopeless!" he moaned.

"It's got to be here somewhere," said Resus. "Try the top shelf."

"I'll do it," said Cleo, dragging a desk across the room and climbing onto it.

"Is it up there?" Luke asked.

"Is WHAT up there?" boomed a voice behind them. The trio spun round to find Dr Skully standing in the doorway. Scapula sat at his feet.

"*Skipstone's Tales of Scream Street*, sir," admitted Cleo, climbing down.

"And why would it be?" questioned the teacher. "Especially when I have explained that Skipstone's writings are worth little, if anything, to the reader?"

"It's Luke, sir!" said Resus. "He's turning into a werewolf again! We were hoping there would be something in the book that would help him."

Dr Skully turned to Luke. "Is this true?" he asked. "Are you in the early stages of your transformation?"

Luke swallowed hard. "Yes, sir," he lied feebly, waving his arms around a little and pretending to growl. "Grrrr!"

The skeleton sighed. "Well, although there is no way to reverse a werewolf transformation, Samuel Skipstone did, apparently, research the subject."

Luke's eyes lit up. "Do you have a copy of his book, sir?" he asked.

"I own the *only* copy," replied the teacher.

"Can we see it?" asked Cleo.

"Unfortunately not," said Dr Skully, shaking his head. "It was confiscated."

"Confiscated?" said Luke. "Who confiscates a book from a teacher?"

Chapter Six
The Hellhounds

"**Sir Otto Sneer?**" asked Luke as he, Resus and Cleo arrived at the gates to a sprawling mansion opposite Everwell's Emporium. A sign read: SNEER HALL.

"The nice man who disconnected your gas supply," said Resus.

"And *he* confiscated *Skipstone's Tales of Scream Street?*"

"He confiscates everything," said Cleo. "Spells, potions, souvenirs. I had a pet hamster until he decided it was against the rules!"

"He does it to keep us in our place," said Resus. "Whenever he thinks we're satisfied with life he just takes stuff from us, or rations it out."

"Like the gas?" asked Luke.

Resus nodded. "My dad says we used to have electricity, too."

"Did he confiscate the sun as well?" said Luke, looking up as a blanket of dark clouds rolled in to obscure the stars. "We're supposed to be on our lunch break but it looks like the middle of the night!"

Resus grinned. "I guess that living in constant night will take a bit of getting used to!"

"Why would Sir Otto want the book?" asked Cleo.

Resus tried the gates; they were locked. "I've no idea, but I don't think he'll be too happy that we've come to ask about it."

Cleo reached up and pulled the bell cord. A window in the mansion flung open with a crash and the landlord appeared, cigar jutting from his mouth.

"What?" he roared.

"Mr Sneer, it's Cleo Farr—"

"SIR Sneer!" thundered the landlord.

"Sorry," said Cleo. "*Sir* Sneer. We were hoping we might be able to take a quick peek at the book you, er … borrowed from Dr Skully recently."

"Who is it?" roared a voice in the background. Luke stared as the face of Sir Otto began to change. The skin pulled tighter and long ginger hair sprouted from the landlord's scalp. Within seconds, Dixon was smiling down at them.

"Fooled you!" he giggled, waving. "It was me all the time!"

"Dixon is Sir Otto's nephew," whispered Resus. "He's a shapeshifter, but not exactly the sharpest fang in the mouth, if you know what I mean!"

Dixon was shoved roughly aside as the real Sir Otto appeared at the window. "Which book are you talking about?" he demanded.

"*Skipstone's Tales of Scream Street*, sir," said Luke. "Can we see it?"

"Certainly not!" bellowed the landlord. "How dare you freaks expect decent, normal people to

share their belongings with the likes of you?" Sir Otto slammed the window and disappeared from view.

"No!" yelled Luke, reaching for the bell again.

Cleo grabbed his arm. "It's no good," she said. "He won't listen."

"But we have to read that book!" said Luke.

"And we will," smiled Resus. "But there's more than one way…" He reached inside his cloak and produced a can of beer.

"I don't know what the law is here in Scream Street," said Luke, "but in my world we're much too young to drink."

"It's not for *us*," said Resus, crouching on the grass beside the path and pulling back the can's ring pull. It opened with a *tshh!* and, almost instantly, a hand with green cracked skin shot out of the soil beneath his feet and grabbed it.

"Brewski!" beamed the zombie as his face appeared. "Cheers, little dude!"

"Doug," said Resus. "We need a favour."

Luke followed the zombie through the tunnel he had dug out for them, delighted that Resus had found a way to get inside the mansion and, at the same time, terrified the earth would collapse around them at any moment.

"Are you sure you little dudes want to visit this place?" asked Doug from the front of the line. "I heard there's some heavy stuff goes on in there!"

"We have to," replied Resus. "Sir Otto's got a book we need to look at."

"Well, if it's in the cause of literature," beamed Doug, satisfied. "You know, I wrote a book once."

Luke smiled. "Amazing," he said. "And I thought zombies were all about killing people and eating brains. What was the book called?"

"*Top 10 Ways to Cook Human Flesh.*"

Resus fought back a laugh as he heard Luke catch his breath.

Doug reached up and burst through the roof of the tunnel. Fresh air flooded Luke's nostrils as the zombie helped him to climb out next to a side door to Sneer Hall.

"Thanks for your help," said Resus.

"Any time, dudes!" grinned the zombie. "Always happy to stick it to the man!" And with a wink he disappeared into the hole, dragging earth over himself.

Resus turned to the door. "Time for a little breaking and entering," he said. He slid a long fingernail into the lock of the door and wiggled it about.

"Will that work?" asked Luke.

"Strong enough to cut glass," grinned Resus. "You just have to be careful not to forget about them and scratch your bum."

With a soft click, the lock released. Resus gripped the handle. "I hope the alarm's not on." He pulled open the door. Silence. "I think we're safe," he said. Then the vampire's smile faltered as a deep-throated growl rang out behind them.

Luke spun round to discover two large black dogs running their way. Fire flickered in their eyes and saliva dripped from their mouths, burning the ground with a hiss. "What," he said, his eyes wide, "are *they*?"

"Hellhounds!" screamed Cleo.

"Quick!" yelled Resus. "Inside!" He pulled Luke and Cleo through the door and slammed it behind them. They were plunged into darkness.

"Where are we?" whispered Cleo.

Luke felt around, knocking over a wooden pole. "I don't know."

The gloom was pierced by the beam of a torch. Resus waved the light. "Look what I found in my pocket," he said.

"I've got to get one of those cloaks," said Cleo.

In the dim light, Luke realized they were in a small store cupboard filled with gardening equipment. The pole he had knocked over was a rake. "This isn't an entrance to the house at all!" he moaned.

The door shook as one of the dogs threw itself at it from the other side. "That lock won't hold out for long," said Cleo. The door rattled again.

"They're not going to give up," said Luke. "What do we do?"

"Can't you transform into your werewolf and fight them off?" asked Resus.

Luke shook his head. "It doesn't work like that. I'd need to be angry and—"

Without a word, Resus swung the torch round and hit him across the head.

"Ow!" yelled Luke. "What did you do that for?"

"I'm trying to make you angry!" said Resus.

"Is this some sort of joke to you?" snapped Luke.

"Of course not," said Resus. "Chill out."

"Chill out?" demanded Luke. "You're trying to change me into the creature that brought my parents here, and you want me to chill out?"

"Luke, I'm sure he didn't mean..." began Cleo.

"Why don't *you* bite them?" demanded Luke. "You're the scary vampire!"

"Please!" begged Cleo. Another thud as the dogs attacked the door.

"'I'll only bite you if you annoy me,' you said. Well, I'm annoying you now, Resus, so either bite me or get out there and bite those dogs!"

"Stop it!" shouted Cleo, grabbing his arm.

Luke shook himself free. "I'll tell you why you're not going to fight those hellhounds," he roared. "It's because you're a coward!"

"No!" yelled Resus. "It's because I'm a normal!"

Luke stared at Resus in the torchlight. "That's not true," he said. "You're a vampire. Your parents ... I've seen them. They're vampires!"

Resus wiped his eyes with his cape, smearing the dark rings around them. It was face paint. "My parents *are* vampires," he said. "I'm some sort of genetic freak. Born with blond hair; you can see my reflection in mirrors ... and the only thing that happens to me in the sunlight is that I get a tan."

"But – your nails!" said Luke. "You picked the lock with your nails!"

Resus held up his hand and showed Luke where the metal fingernails fitted over his own.

 63

"Fake," he said. "Just like these." Reaching into his mouth, the vampire unclipped his fangs and took them out.

"I-I didn't know," said Luke.

"I try to be scary," said Resus quietly. "I try to act threatening so that people won't know the truth, but it's no use. I'm not a real vampire at all!"

The hellhounds continued to throw themselves at the door.

"Then there's only one way out," said Luke, picking up the rake. "We fight."

Chapter Seven
The Library

The door burst open, hitting one of the hellhounds and knocking it off balance. Luke leapt out, twirling the rake as if it were a staff. He swung it round, catching the legs of the other dog and sending it tumbling.

Resus followed, wielding a shovel that he brought down on the first dog's head as it

staggered to its feet. It crumpled back to the ground, whining.

The second hellhound barked, fire raging in its eyes. It lunged for Resus, but Cleo jumped in its way and knocked it to one side with a metal dustbin lid. The trio stood firm, makeshift weapons raised, as the hellhounds shook their heads and snarled.

"If we can push them back, we might be able to get round to the main doors," said Luke.

"We'd better hope they're not locked," said Resus, "or we'll be just as trapped there."

Luke nodded. "One of us should go and find a way in while the other two keep these things occupied."

"I'll do it!" shouted Cleo, dropping her dustbin lid and running off.

Resus grabbed for her bandages but she was moving too fast. "She never learns!" he groaned. He snatched the dustbin lid from the ground and used it to hold the dogs at bay.

The two hellhounds split up, advancing from either side and forcing Luke and Resus to stand back-to-back. One of the hounds darted for Luke, teeth bared. Luke swung the rake around, catching the dog in the throat.

Its companion howled with rage and leapt forward, its front paws shoving Luke to the ground. The dog scraped a claw across his face, scratching his cheek and drawing blood. Luke tried to hit it with the

rake but his arms were trapped beneath the hell-hound's back legs. He was pinned down.

The dog growled down at Luke, deadly saliva threatening to drip into his eyes at any moment. As it lunged for his throat, Resus swung the dustbin lid at the creature's face. The dog fell to the grass, howling with pain.

"Thanks," said Luke as Resus helped him to his feet.

"Any time," replied the vampire, keeping his eyes on the dogs as they approached again. One of the hellhounds reared up onto its back legs and Resus was forced to hold the dustbin lid out like a shield to protect himself.

The dog dropped down, spotting the reflection of Cleo running for the doors in the shiny metal lid. Barking a warning, it turned and raced after the fleeing mummy, its companion following.

"Cleo!" bellowed Luke.

Cleo turned to see the dogs on her tail and picked up speed, her feet pounding against the grass as she ran. She could hear the growling of the hellhounds as they got closer, and she fixed her gaze on the doors ahead. She had to reach them. Had to get inside.

The first dog pounced and landed squarely on Cleo's back, pushing her to the ground and ripping at her bandages. The second dog grabbed her foot between its teeth and bit down.

Cleo screamed as acidic saliva burned into her skin. She tried to crawl away but the dogs pulled her back, nipping and scratching at her; toying with their prey before they destroyed it.

Luke and Resus ran as fast as they could towards the mummy, knowing they had only seconds to save her from the rabid hounds.

Luke raised the rake into the air and brought it down hard onto the dog at Cleo's throat. It yelped as the metal prongs pierced its flesh. Resus hit it with his shovel, and the dog collapsed to one side, unconscious.

The second dog pulled back its lips and snarled angrily at the boys. Resus snorted back a laugh. "You're not the only one with teeth!" he shouted.

The young vampire turned his eyes upwards until only the whites were visible. Opening his mouth wide, he licked the tips of his fake fangs and hissed. The hellhound yelped in terror and raced away across the flower-beds.

Luke dropped to his knees beside Cleo. Her bandages were ripped and burnt by the dog's drool. She wasn't moving.

Cleo opened her eyes. She was lying on a plush couch in a room built of iron and glass. Plants filled every available space.

A face appeared among the foliage: Resus. "Morning, sleepy!" he joked.

Cleo sat up, wincing as a throbbing sensation filled her skull. She touched a tender lump on her forehead.

"You hit your head on a rock when the dog pounced," explained Resus. "Knocked yourself out cold. We thought it was a lot worse for a moment, though."

Cleo looked down at her bandages. Some of them were missing and had been replaced with strips of silky red material. "What happened?" she asked.

"Your bandages were covered with that acid the dogs were drooling. We had to get them off before they burned your skin too badly."

Cleo ran her fingers over the red material. "Wait, this is the lining of your cape," she said.

 70

Resus shrugged. "What do I need it for? Only real vampires have capes."

Cleo scowled. "You *are* a real vampire, Resus!"

"He certainly is," said Luke, pushing his way through a small jungle of plant life. "You should have seen the way he scared off that hellhound!"

Cleo stood, testing her leg. It ached when she put any pressure on it, but at least she was able to walk. "Where are we?" she asked.

"Sir Otto's conservatory," said Luke. "The front doors were locked, but we found an open window here. It wasn't easy getting you through it. Have you ever thought about going on a diet?" Cleo slapped him playfully on the arm.

"Did you find anything?" asked Resus.

"No sign of the book yet," replied Luke, "but there is something rather interesting out in the corridor…"

Luke, Resus and Cleo gazed up at the portrait of the vampire.

"That," said Luke, "looks like you!"

"It does," agreed Cleo.

"It's my ancestor," explained Resus. "Count Negatov."

"Wasn't he one of the first residents of Scream Street?" asked Cleo.

Resus nodded. "He was forced out of Transylvania and came here to build Scream Street, along with the other founding fathers. My dad told me about him."

"Sounds like your family and Sir Otto's go back a long way," grinned Luke. "You sure you can't just go up—"

"Someone's coming!" hissed Cleo, quickly pulling Luke and Resus into a gap behind a nearby sideboard. Sir Otto's nephew, Dixon, appeared at the end of the corridor, singing to himself: "You put your left arm in, your left arm out…"

"He's coming this way!" said Cleo.

Luke searched for a better hiding place. There was a doorway opposite, but no way of crossing to it without being spotted. They needed a diversion.

Dixon paused to pull faces at himself in a mirror and Luke saw his chance. He grabbed a vase from the sideboard and hurled it along the corridor. It soared through the air over Dixon's head and hit a suit of armour.

The armour swayed to one side then back

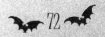

72

again, crashing down on top of Dixon. He screamed. "Help! It's attacking me! Help!"

Luke darted across the corridor and opened the door. He, Resus and Cleo hurried inside, closing it behind them. They found themselves in a richly decorated room lined with bookshelves.

"I guess this is the library," said Resus.

"Well," said Luke, "if the book's anywhere, it will be in here."

"Right," said Resus. "Let's start searching."

"Not again!" moaned Cleo. "We'll be here all nigh—"

The door to the library crashed open and Dixon entered, his arms piled high with pieces of armour. "I'm telling you, Uncle Otto, it jumped on top of me!"

Luke and Resus ducked under a large desk as Cleo dropped to the floor and slid beneath a leather couch.

Sir Otto entered the room behind Dixon, cigar clamped firmly between his lips. "Jumped on top of you, indeed! You're a waste of DNA!"

Resus nudged Luke and pointed to a silver-backed book the landlord was carrying. "That's it," he mouthed. *"Skipstone's Tales of Scream Street!"*

Dixon dropped the armour onto the floor with a clatter.

"Be careful!" roared the landlord. "That armour is centuries old."

"You should get new stuff, then, Uncle Otto," said Dixon. "Something with silver sequins – or purple to match your face when you get angry!"

"Don't be cheeky!"

Sir Otto waddled over to one of the shelves and pulled a book out of its place. There was a click and a whirr as a doorway in the shelves slid open. The landlord disappeared through it. Dixon remained in the library.

"How's it going with the book, Uncle?" he called.

"It's not!" said the landlord. "The stupid thing still hasn't told me anything."

"Do you want me to try?" asked Dixon. "I like books!"

Sir Otto reappeared without the book, the doorway closing behind him. "The only books you can cope with are the kind you have to colour in," he sneered.

"That's not fair!" Dixon's lower lip trembled

74

as he followed his uncle out of the library. "I like comics, too!"

As the door closed, Luke, Resus and Cleo climbed to their feet.

"We have to get into that secret room," said Luke. "Then we can find out what Samuel Skipstone wrote about how to leave Scream Street."

Chapter Eight
The Book

Luke pulled out book after book, trying to remember which title Sir Otto had moved to trigger the secret door. He reached the end of the shelf, but nothing had happened.

"This is ridiculous!" he snapped. "I know it was one of these!" He kicked out angrily, stubbing his toe against the shelves. Pain shot through

his foot and he dropped onto a nearby couch to pull off his trainer and massage the injury.

"That hurtsh!" he hissed.

"Hurtsh?" repeated Resus. "Have your lips stopped working?"

Luke shrugged. "It jusht came out like—"

Another bolt of pain hit him, this time shooting through his face as his upper jaw splintered and pushed outwards to create a wolf's snout. A long tongue lolled out of his mouth and thick whiskers sprouted from either side of his nose.

"Oh, thish ish jusht fantashtic!" he moaned, running his fingers over the length of his dog-like features.

"You sound just like me when I first got these clip-on fangs!" giggled Resus.

"That shkunk inshide your cloak ish decomposhing fasht," grumbled Luke, sniffing at the air with his new, sensitive nose. He smiled as another scent filled his nostrils. "I can shmell Shir Shneer!"

Cleo shook her head. "Nope," she said, "didn't get a word of that!"

"Otto Shneer!" said Luke, wiping strings of drool from his chin. "I've picked up hish schent!"

 77

"Oh!" exclaimed Cleo. "I can smell him too; those cigars really pong."

"It'sh not the shigarsh I can shmell," slavered Luke. "I can shee the booksh he wash touching!" He sniffed the row of books, following the landlord's scent.

"Thish one," he announced. "And hish fingersh only touched the firsht two shentimetres." He carefully pulled the book out a short way. There was a click, and the unit slid inwards to reveal a dark passageway beyond.

Resus grinned. "Shuper-duper!"

Luke's face shrank back as he led the way down a stone staircase.

"Doesn't that hurt?" asked Cleo.

"Like you wouldn't believe," replied Luke. "But it's proving helpful."

"We need a little light on the situation," said Resus. He reached inside his cloak and pulled out a length of wood that crackled with fire at one end.

Cleo stared. "Why would you have a flaming torch inside your cloak?"

Resus shrugged. "I lost the battery-operated one fighting the hellhounds."

In the flickering torchlight, Luke, Resus and Cleo examined Sir Otto's secret room. Both the walls and the floor were of simple, bare stone. A series of wires and metal clamps pushed through one of the walls.

"What are these?" asked Cleo, studying a vice that jutted out.

"I've no idea," said Resus. "But I know what that is!" Following his gaze, Luke and Cleo saw *Skipstone's Tales of Scream Street* sitting on top of a stone pillar.

Luke reached out to take it, but as his hand touched the book it was surrounded by a ball of white light. He yelped and pulled his fingers back.

"What's the matter?" asked Resus.

"It gave me a shock!" exclaimed Luke, sucking his fingertips.

Resus smiled. "I'll get it," he said. Within seconds the vampire was also nursing a jolted hand as the ball of light wrapped itself around the book again.

"I've not come this far to walk away now," said Luke, reaching out with his other hand. There was a crackle and he spun away, cursing.

Resus tried again with his uninjured hand.
Soon both boys were hopping round the room,
fingers jammed into their armpits.

"Are you both brain-dead?" Cleo asked. "It's
obviously some sort of energy shield. Whenever
you reach out for the book, the shield activates
and zaps you."

"And what do you suggest we do about it?" asked Luke.

"Leave it to mummy!" Cleo grinned. She unwrapped the bandages from her right arm. The skin beneath was black and wrinkled, like burnt chicken. She reached out and grabbed hold of the book. The energy shield fizzed into life and Cleo gritted her teeth against the pain as she lifted the tome off its pillar.

"Boys!" she said.

School had finished for the day and Luke, Resus and Cleo now sat on the floor in Resus's bedroom. The book lay on the carpet between them, the face of a man raised up from its silver cover.

A variety of fierce-looking weapons were hung by lengths of wire from the ceiling above them, and on the pillow of Resus's bed was a teddy in a cape with its head missing. The walls were splashed with what Luke hoped was red paint.

"What do we do now?" asked Cleo.

"We read," said Luke. He grabbed the book and opened it at a random page. It showed a recipe for gnome stew. The following page advertised disguise kits for germs, while the next was

taken up with a rousing poem about toenails. Everything was written in the same, scrawled handwriting.

A feeling of hopelessness began to wash over Luke as he flicked faster and faster through the pages. The book had absolutely nothing in it that could help him open a doorway home. Luke threw it to the floor.

"We went through all that and the book's useless!" he moaned.

"I wouldn't say useless…" said a voice. Luke glanced up at Resus and Cleo, but neither of them had spoken. Cautiously he turned the book over.

The face on the cover now had its eyes open and it was smiling. "Thank you. I have a dust allergy, and this carpet hasn't been vacuumed for a while."

"We don't have any electricity," said Resus slowly, not quite certain if he should be talking to a book. "We have to rely on the spiders to clean up."

"Ah yes, the electricity," said the face. "I know all about that."

"Excuse me," said Cleo, "but who *are* you?"

The silver face grinned. "Where are my

82

manners?" it exclaimed. "Samuel Skipstone –
author of *Skipstone's Tales of Scream Street*!"

"You wrote this book?" asked Luke.

"Wrote the book?" beamed Skipstone. "I *am*
the book!" He gazed at the surprised faces around
him, then sighed.

"This bit always confuses people," he said.
"Most authors write their books and then their
involvement ends. But I was so engrossed in my
work that, as I lay dying, I used a spell to merge
my spirit with the pages."

"So you're trapped in there?" asked Cleo.

"Trapped?" replied Skipstone. "Not at all!

I am here by choice!"

"But the pages, I mean *your* pages, are filled with silly things like poems and sketches," said Resus. "There's nothing serious about Scream Street in it at all."

Samuel Skipstone winked. "What better place to hide important knowledge than among useless claptrap? I do not discuss my work with just anyone."

"So you haven't told Sir Otto what you know?" asked Luke.

"Nor will I," answered Skipstone. "I do not approve of Sneer's plans for Scream Street. I have remained mute at his every question."

"I heard Sir Otto say you hadn't told him anything," said Luke. "I thought he just hadn't found what he was looking for, but he must have meant you weren't speaking!"

Skipstone nodded. "However, for three such eager young minds, I am prepared to talk. Ask and I shall answer!"

Luke took a deep breath. "I want to leave Scream Street."

Samuel Skipstone fixed Luke with his silvery eyes. "And why would a werewolf want to leave

 84

the place where he can live among those who accept him?"

Cleo gasped. "You can tell that Luke is a werewolf?"

"I am something of an expert on the subject of lycanthropy," said the author. "There are ways of knowing a werewolf when you see one."

"It's not for me," continued Luke. "It's for my mum and dad." He told Samuel Skipstone about how his family had arrived in Scream Street. He explained how scared his parents were and how, even though he had made friends here, he didn't want to put his parents through the ordeal any longer.

When Luke had finished speaking, Skipstone remained quiet for a moment, then spoke softly. "It is a noble quest to leave the place where you belong for the sake of those you love. I will help all I can."

"You'll tell me how to take my parents home?" exclaimed Luke.

"It is not that simple," replied Skipstone. "Only the six founding fathers of Scream Street have the power to make such a thing possible."

"Founding fathers?" said Cleo. "Like Count Negatov?"

"Indeed," said Skipstone. "Allow me to introduce them..."

Chapter Nine
The Clue

The silver book flicked open to a page containing an article about basic gargoyle maintenance. Luke, Resus and Cleo watched as the handwritten words faded away and an illustration took their place.

The picture showed a street party with figures sitting around a long table, eating and laughing. As Luke watched, the image began to move. There was no sound except the scratch of pencil on paper as the illustration was constantly redrawn, but it was obvious that everyone was having a great deal of fun.

"That's Scream Street!" he said.

"It can't be," said Cleo. "The sun's out!"

"The sun used to shine every day," explained Skipstone. "It is only recently that the sky has been veiled in darkness."

A vampire stood at the head of the table and raised a glass. "Count Negatov!" exclaimed Resus. "The first vampire in Scream Street!"

"These are the founding fathers and their families," said the author.

"What are they celebrating?" asked Cleo as the vampire's silent toast was greeted with equally noise-free applause.

"The completion of Scream Street," said Skipstone. "The electricity generator had just been put in place. No longer would the residents have to cook and heat their homes with dangerous gas."

Resus glanced up at the flickering flame that

barely lit his bedroom. "Doesn't look like we've come very far," he commented.

The picture faded and the scrawled article came back into view. "The founding fathers can give you the power to see your greatest wish realized," said Skipstone.

"You mean like opening a doorway back to my world?" asked Luke.

"If that is your desire, then yes," said the author.

"But surely everyone in that picture is long gone," said Cleo.

"Very true," replied Skipstone.

Luke's heart sank. "Then we're stuck here!"

"Do not dismiss the founding fathers so quickly," said Skipstone. "They all left behind something to help those who came after."

"What do you mean?" asked Cleo.

"They each donated something very personal," said the author. "Once collected, these relics will provide the finder with their combined power."

"What's a relic?" asked Cleo.

"It's like a souvenir," explained Resus. "Something you use to remember something or someone."

Cleo smiled. "So all we have to do is find these six relics and Luke can open a doorway home?" she asked. "That doesn't sound too hard."

"It might not be that simple," answered Skipstone. "The relics are hidden well, and only clues were left to their true locations. They must also be collected in the exact order in which they were donated."

"It can't be impossible, though," said Luke. "They were left behind to help people. To give them the power of the founding fathers."

"Indeed," said the author. "However, they could easily be misused. You must ensure the relics do not fall into the wrong hands."

"You mean…"

Samuel Skipstone's voice was solemn. "Sir Otto Sneer! I would imagine his plans for this community are very dark indeed. If he regains possession of me, your family will never leave Scream Street."

"I'll be careful," promised Luke.

Skipstone smiled. "Then allow me to reveal the location of the first relic."

The book flipped open once more. Spidery handwriting dissolved from the page, revealing a hidden portion of text:

In the tunnel, through the slime,
the vampire lies for all of time;
down where all is constant night,
the source of power here will bite

"There's only one kind of slimy tunnel round here," said Resus. "The sewer. There's a trap-door in our cellar that leads down there."

"Then that's where we're going," said Luke. "Do we need to—"

"WHICH ONE OF YOU FREAKS STOLE MY BOOK?"

Sir Otto's voice echoed along Scream Street. Luke, Resus and Cleo dashed to the window. They could just see the landlord standing in the central square, Dixon at his side.

"I guess he's figured out he's one talking book short," said Resus.

Sir Otto bit down hard on his cigar and stroked the silk scarf at his neck. "I know you monsters stick together," he roared, "but if one of you has the guts to come out and tell me who has my book, you shall be spared!"

"Spared from what?" asked Cleo.

"I don't know," replied Resus, "but I don't like the look of *that*."

As the trio watched, Dixon uncoiled a length of wire from the gates of Sneer Hall and attached it to a plunger at Sir Otto's feet.

"You have until the count of ten!" yelled the landlord. "Ten, nine, eight …"

"It's a bomb!" whispered Cleo.

Luke shook his head. "I don't think so. That wire leads back into Sneer Hall. He wouldn't blow up his own mansion."

"… three, two, one!" Sir Otto gripped the handles of the plunger. "Don't say I didn't warn you, Scream Street!" He pushed down hard. Instantly there was a rush of wind and objects began to fly around Resus's bedroom.

Cleo jumped to avoid a falling axe as the wires tethering it to the ceiling snapped. "It's a poltergeist attack!" she said. "He's started another attack!"

"That's impossible," said Resus. "You can't control poltergeists!"

"Sneer's obviously found a way," said Luke. "I need to get to my mum and dad; make sure they're OK this time."

Resus grabbed his arm. "Are you crazy? If you go out there, the book will be torn from your hands by the poltergeist! Sir Otto will have it back in no time."

"So what do we do?"

"We start searching for the relics right now," said Resus. "The sooner your parents are away from all of this, the better."

As Luke and Resus made for the bedroom door, a squeal and a thump from behind stopped them in their tracks. The boys turned. Cleo was lying on the floor, a sword that had been hanging from the ceiling buried deep in her chest.

"Cleo!" shouted Resus, kneeling beside her.

The mummy's eyes flickered open. "That stings," she moaned, reaching up to pull the blade from her ribcage.

"Stings?" said Luke. "You should be dead! It went right through your heart!"

"I don't think so," said Cleo, handing the sword to Resus and rearranging her bandages to cover the hole. "My heart is in a golden casket in my bedroom."

"What?" exclaimed Luke. "How?"

"I'm a mummy!" said Cleo. "We have our internal organs removed before we're buried in our tombs. Didn't you do history at school?"

Standing, she stretched to ease the discomfort of the wound, then headed for the door. "Well?" she said. "Are we going down to the sewers, or not?"

Before either boy could reply, Cleo had left the room.

*   *   *

Resus pulled open the trapdoor and thrust the flaming torch into the hole. Luke was just able to make out the ground below. "You're sure this is it?"

"It's the only slime-coated tunnel I know of." Resus climbed down the short ladder, landing in a puddle with a splash. Luke followed.

"I'm going to have to find a new bandage supplier now I've met you," groaned Cleo as she joined them in the mud.

"I'll send you a box once I've opened a doorway home," grinned Luke. "Now, which way do we go?" He looked up and down the sewer tunnel.

"If I was hunting for a vampire, I'd go as deep as possible," said Resus.

"Down it is, then," said Luke, leading the way into the darkness. At each junction, Luke, Resus and Cleo followed the tunnel that led deeper below ground.

After a while they found themselves in a vast underground cavern. Green moss clung to the walls and gave off an eerie glow.

"Gutweed," explained Resus, tucking the

95

torch back inside his cloak. "They used to use it to light children's bedrooms at night."

"I can't imagine sleeping with that stuff in my room," said Luke. "It stinks!"

There was a crash as Cleo knocked something over in the dim light. Reaching down, she picked up a piece of broken dinner plate. "What's this doing here?" she asked.

The trio explored the cavern. Piles of books, clothing, toys and more lay around. Thousands of household objects were stacked from floor to ceiling, the luminous gutweed clinging to everything.

"This is all the stuff Sir Otto's confiscated over the years!" said Resus.

"Well, it's probably ruined now," said Luke. "It'll stink after spending so much time down here. I'm not sure I'll be able to get rid of the pong myself!"

"That's not the gutweed," said Resus. "That smells like—"

A rasping noise made him look up. "Oh, no."

Luke squinted in the half-light. Hundreds of tiny creatures were watching the trio with

dull black eyes. "What," he asked, "are *they*?"

Resus pinched his nose as the vile smell got stronger. "Goblins!"

Chapter Ten
The Great Guff

The goblins crept towards them, leathery feet slapping against the bare stone of the floor. The nearer the creatures got, the fouler the smell became.

Luke pressed a hand over his nose and mouth. "What *is* that?"

"It's what makes goblins so delightful to be around," replied Cleo.

As if on cue, one of the goblins let rip a huge burst of gas from its bottom. The creature was propelled across the cavern, a cloud of green vapour trailing behind. It landed at Luke's feet and planted its hands firmly on its hips.

"I be Squiffer," it announced. "I be demand you no touch goblin 'longings!"

Resus grabbed the goblin and lifted it up to his face. "These *'longings*," he snarled, "have all been stolen by Sir Otto Sneer!"

Squiffer wriggled in Resus's hands. "Flabby man give 'longings to goblins."

"But they belong to the residents of Scream Street!"

"If pointy tooth cannot keep 'longings for himself," jeered Squiffer, "goblins will keep 'longings instead!"

Resus tightened his grip. "How about I show you just how pointy these teeth really are?" he hissed.

The goblin squealed and let out another blast of gas. "Don't be hurt Squiffer! Squiffer can be pointy tooth's friend!"

"That's better," said Resus as the stench subsided. "Now, we're not here for your 'longings.

We're looking for a relic. Something left behind by a vampire. Do you know where it is?"

Squiffer pulled a determined face. "Squiffer be not tell!"

"I thought you said you were going to be his friend?" said Cleo.

The goblin stuck his tongue out at her. "Squiffer be change his mind. Squiffer be complicated that way!"

"Then who *will* tell us?" asked Resus. "Who's in charge here?"

"You be mean head of family?"

"Yes, I mean the head of the family!" snapped Resus. "Who is it?"

Squiffer nodded his head, moving it slower and slower until the nod became a violent shake. "I be no tell you that the Great Guff is head of family!" The goblin clamped a hand across its mouth, eyes wide as it realized it had given the secret away.

"I've had enough of this," said Luke. He snatched the creature from Resus and held it high. "I am a werewolf!" he shouted. "If the Great Guff does not reveal himself to me, I will transform and tear this goblin to pieces!"

Squiffer squealed and pumped out another noxious green cloud, forcing Luke to hold his breath. A larger goblin approached through the mist, wearing woollen baby booties and a cape made from tin foil.

"I be the Great Guff," the goblin announced. "Release Squiffer!"

Luke dropped the squirming creature. Before it hit the ground, it let out another rip of gas that propelled it across the cave. The terrified goblin raced out into the sewer tunnel, screaming.

"You be want 'longing of way old pointy tooth?" asked the Great Guff.

"Yes," Luke said, "we want 'longing of way old pointy tooth. Where is it?"

"That be not the right question," said the goblin. "Right question be what you give the Great Guff first?"

"You want me to give you something for telling me where the vampire's relic is?" Luke asked. The Great Guff smiled and held out his hand.

Luke clenched his fists. "But I don't have anything to give!"

The Great Guff turned away from Luke and folded his arms. "If wolf-boy be getting angry, the Great Guff be no tell!"

"I'm not angry," replied Luke, stuffing his hands into his pockets. "I just…" A smile spread across his face. "I just had to make sure you deserved my present. It can only be given to a great leader – if you know of one, that is."

The Great Guff gasped. "*I* be great leader! I be the Great Guff!"

"What a coincidence," said Luke, pulling the dog's collar from his pocket. The silver buckle glinted in the soft light. "Then this must be for you."

"What be that?" asked the Great Guff.

"This is a valuable necklace," said Luke. "Do you want it?"

The goblin watched the collar swing with greedy eyes. "Yes!" it breathed excitedly. "Give 'longing to the Great Guff!"

"OK," said Luke, "but there's one tiny adjustment to make." He turned to Resus. "I don't suppose you have a marker pen inside that cloak, do you?"

The vampire grinned. "A marker pen? Why, this is a virtual stationery cupboard!" He reached inside his cape and hunted for the pen, handing Cleo a bicycle wheel and a toaster to hold while he dug deep into the pockets.

Eventually he produced a black felt-tip pen with a flourish. Luke took it and changed the name on the dog collar's tag from FLUFFY to GUFFY.

"Your Majesty," said Luke, bowing as he held out the collar. But the goblin's eyes were now fixed on something far more interesting: Resus's cloak.

"Why be the Great Guff want necklace when the Great Guff be having pointy tooth's cloak?" he said.

"I don't like the sound of this…" began Luke.

"Many 'longings in pointy tooth's cloak!"

"No! We agreed—"

"Goblins! Get 'longings!" screamed the Great Guff. Bearing razor-sharp teeth, the pack of

goblins attacked. Within seconds, Luke, Resus and Cleo were overwhelmed by the tiny farting monsters.

Luke kicked one of the goblins in the stomach. It flew across the cavern, squealing as it crashed into a pile of board games and books. Another goblin instantly took its place, grabbing Luke's leg and biting hard.

Cleo was forced to the ground by the creatures as they rasped green fumes in her face. She pulled her bandages up to cover her mouth, but the dressing offered little protection and she felt her consciousness begin to slip away.

Resus pulled a golf club from his cloak and used it to drive the goblins away. "Fore!" he shouted as he whacked the creatures across the cave. But for every goblin he dispatched, three more leapt at him and soon he, too, was covered in the stinking, pumping creatures.

The green gas erupting from the goblins now enveloped Luke completely. Through streaming eyes he tried to locate his friends, but all he could see was even more goblins as they jumped on top of him.

"Resus!" he shouted. "Where are you?"

 104

"Here!" yelled the vampire, biting into a goblin's bottom with his fangs and getting a cloud of green fumes in his face for his trouble.

"Cover your eyes!" called Luke in reply. "Cleo, you too!"

Cleo and Resus had no choice but to comply. They yanked their hands away from their goblin attackers and pressed them over their eyes as Luke lunged over to where he had heard Resus's voice.

Luke thrust his hand inside Resus's cape and

pulled out the flaming torch. Screwing his own eyes tight shut, he plunged the torch deep into the centre of the goblin gas cloud.

The cavern exploded.

When Luke opened his eyes, his first thought was of amazement that he could still operate any part of his body at all. The explosion had been far bigger than he had expected and his ears were still ringing from the blast.

"Luke Watson," moaned Cleo as she came round and forced herself into a sitting position. "Since I met you I've been burnt, stabbed and now blown up... This is the best fun I've had in centuries!"

"My hair's all burnt at the ends," complained Resus.

"Serves you right for dyeing it so much, doesn't it," teased Cleo. "I knew that spray-on stuff wasn't good for you!"

"How do you know about that?"

"Resus, *everyone* knows," replied Cleo. "It's the worst-kept secret in Scream Street!" The vampire pulled a sulky face.

"Your hair *is* burnt a bit, though," said Luke,

reaching out to touch it. "Hey, is that a bald patch?"

The vampire slapped his hand away. "My fangs are still in full working order," he warned.

"Looks like the goblins came off worse," said Cleo. The tiny creatures were scattered across the floor of the cavern, an occasional *eep!* of green gas the only sign they were still alive.

"We'd better get out of here before they wake up," said Resus.

"Look!" whispered Luke. In the centre of the cave, clearly visible now the goblins' stash of stolen items had been blown away, was a stone coffin.

"Do you think that's where the relic is?" asked Cleo, climbing to her feet.

Resus shrugged. "I guess we'll have to open it to be sure."

"I'll do it!" yelled Cleo, skipping across the cavern.

"And, somehow, it's always her that gets hurt…" grinned Resus as he and Luke followed the mummy.

The trio gathered beside the coffin and pushed at the stone lid. A scraping echoed around the cave as it shifted slightly.

 107

"It's too heavy," said Luke. "We need something like a—"

"Crowbar?" asked Resus, pulling a long metal tool from his cloak.

Luke grinned. "It's no wonder the goblins are fans of your wardrobe!"

Using the crowbar they were able to slide the heavy lid across the top of the coffin. Straining against the weight, Luke, Resus and Cleo pushed with all their might until gravity took over and the slab of stone crashed to the floor.

The perfectly preserved body of a vampire lay inside, enshrouded in a black silk cloak. Resus gasped.

"It's Count Negatov!"

Chapter Eleven
The Fang

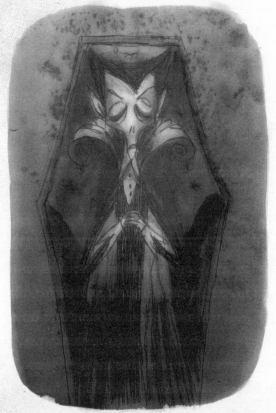

"I was only expecting the relic," said Luke. "Not the vampire himself."

"Is he dead?" asked Cleo, nudging Count Negatov's cheek with her finger.

"If he isn't, he'll have one heck of a stiff back when he gets up," said Resus. "According to the carvings on the coffin, he's been down here for over a century."

"Come on," said Luke, "let's find this relic and get out of here."

"I don't know…" said Cleo. "It feels weird going through a dead vampire's pockets."

A cloud of gas appeared as one of the goblins rolled over and let rip.

"Maybe you'd prefer to wait until these guys wake up so you can ask them for help?" suggested Resus.

Cleo frowned. "Let's do it."

Luke lifted the edge of Count Negatov's cape and he, Cleo and Resus slid their hands inside, exploring the cloak's many pockets.

"I've got something," said Luke. He pulled out a piece of parchment and unfurled it. "It looks like a family tree."

"Vampires are buried with details of their ancestors," explained Resus. "So that they can be easily identified in the next life."

"That doesn't help us find the relic," said Luke. "It's not here."

"Read the clue again," suggested Cleo.

Luke pulled *Skipstone's Tales of Scream Street* out of his pocket and opened it. The trio gathered around the book and read:

In the tunnel, through the slime,
the vampire lies for all of time;
down where all is constant night,
the source of power here will bite

"It's his fangs," said Resus.

"Fangs?" asked Luke. "Are you sure?"

"The source of power here will bite," read Resus aloud. "The only part of a vampire that bites is his fangs."

"We have to take his teeth?" asked Cleo, disgusted.

Resus nodded. "It's the one thing that only a vampire can leave behind."

Luke stretched out his hand and carefully pushed back Count Negatov's top lip. The vampire's fangs glowed in the light of the gutweed. Luke took one of them between his fingers and pulled gently. It was stuck fast.

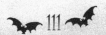

"Shame he's not wearing dentures, like you," Luke said. "There's no way they're coming out."

"Try this," suggested Resus, producing a pair of pliers from his cloak.

Cleo looked horrified. "You can't be serious!"

"Have you got any better ideas?" asked Resus. "We've got to do something before the farting army here wakes up."

Luke took the pliers and clamped hold of one of Count Negatov's fangs. "Do we need both of them?" he asked.

Resus shook his head. "A vampire needs his fangs to feed in the next life, so we'd better leave him one."

"Right," said Luke. "You two hold his head down and I'll pull."

Cleo and Resus positioned themselves at the top of the coffin and pressed their hands against the dead vampire's head. Cleo turned away, unable to watch.

"The good news," beamed Resus, "is that he's been dead for over a century, so there shouldn't be any blood."

Cleo kicked him in the shin. "You're enjoying this!" she snapped.

"Right," said Luke. "On three. One … two … three!"

In one swift movement, Cleo and Resus pushed down on the vampire's head as Luke gripped the pliers and pulled. With a sickening crack, the fang came free. A fountain of blood spurted from Count Negatov's mouth.

"You said there wouldn't be any blood!" Cleo squealed.

"There shouldn't be!" shouted Resus. "When vampires die, their blood evaporates. I don't understand it!"

As Luke held up the tooth to examine it, a hand shot out of the coffin and grabbed his throat. "I think I know why there's blood…" he gurgled.

"Who dares to disturb my rest?" demanded the vampire in a deep, solemn voice. His eyes were wide open, staring up at the children.

Luke swallowed hard. The vampire's grip on his throat was closing tighter. "My name is Luke Watson," he said in a strangled voice. "S–Samuel Skipstone sent me."

Count Negatov's eyes narrowed. "How do I know you speak the truth?"

Resus darted round the coffin until he was in the vampire's line of sight. "Count Negatov," he said. "I am Resus Negative, descendant of the glorious Negatov dynasty." He held his hand out towards the vampire.

Count Negatov studied the lines crossing Resus's palm. "You are indeed of the Negatov line," he said. "But who is he that has taken my fang?"

"He's a werewolf," explained Resus. "I'm helping him to collect the six relics of the founding fathers so that he can take his family out of Scream Street."

Count Negatov sighed. "For over a hundred years I have slept, awaiting the moment my relic would be collected. I have but one question…" The vampire stared deep into Luke's eyes and asked, "Is he worthy of this gift?"

Resus smiled. "Yes, sire. He's my friend!"

The vampire released his grip on Luke's throat. "Then I may finally pass on to the next life," he said. "Your quest has received the blessing of the vampires."

Count Negatov closed his eyes for the final time and was silent.

Luke, Resus and Cleo made their way back along the sewer tunnel, the flickering torch illuminating the fang as Luke studied it.

"Thank you," he said to Resus for the fifth time in as many minutes.

"It's no problem," said Resus. "You'd have done the same for me."

"Sorry to disturb such a touching moment,"

said Cleo, "but can we please get out of here so I can wash at least some of these stains out of my bandages?"

Luke grinned at her in the torchlight. "I think you look rather fetching," he said. "I hear mud brown and gutweed green are the in colours this season."

"If I wasn't so nice..." began Cleo. She stopped. "Shh! What's that?"

"What?" said Luke. "I can't hear anything."

"It's like wind," said Cleo. "Wind that's squeaking!"

Resus's cape flapped and he struggled to keep hold of the torch as some unseen force threatened to pull it from his hands. "It's a poltergeist!" he shouted.

"Then what's squeaking?" asked Luke. The answer came as dozens of rats flew along the tunnel towards them, swept up by the poltergeist's power.

One of them gripped Luke's cheek as it bounced past, digging its claws into his skin to try to anchor itself. "Get it off me!" Luke yelled.

Resus reached inside his cloak and pulled out the first thing he could find: the crowbar. He

  116

swung it towards Luke's head, knocking the rat away but hitting his friend in the process.

"Ow!"

"Sorry!" Resus apologized.

"That really hurt!" said Luke, rubbing at his cheek. He pulled his hand away as blood began to run down his fingertips.

"That rat must have scratched you," said Cleo.

"No," said Luke. "It's not the rat." He gazed down at his fingernails as they stretched and grew, curling over to form powerful claws. "I'm changing!"

"Will it stop with your hands?" asked Resus. "I don't fancy being trapped underground with an angry werewolf!" The flaming torch was ripped from his hand. It clattered away down the tunnel, plunging the trio into blackness.

"Strike that," he shouted against the roar of the wind. "I don't fancy being trapped underground *in the dark* with an angry werewolf!"

The poltergeist attack was building. Rocks, twigs and clumps of mud swirled around the confines of the tunnel.

"Hold on to me!" yelled Luke, digging his claws into the wall of the sewer pipe. Resus

gripped Luke's belt and offered Cleo the edge of his cloak to hold. The ends of the mummy's bandages flapped out behind her.

Hand over hand, Luke dug his claws into the brickwork of the tunnel, dragging himself and his friends back towards the trapdoor. "I didn't think the poltergeist's effects could be felt in the sewer!"

"Maybe someone knows we're down here," shouted Resus in reply.

"Impossible!" yelled Cleo. "Who could have told Sir Otto where we are?"

Luke glanced over his shoulder. "Squiffer?"

"I've got a nice big cork in my cape," said the vampire. "I'll bung up his bum for good, once we get out of here!"

The trio finally reached the ladder that led up to the cellar. As Luke climbed, the trapdoor opened and he found himself staring into a familiar face. "Dr Skully?"

"I thought you might need a hand with Skipstone's quest," the skeleton said.

Dr Skully reached down and helped Cleo to clamber past the boys and out of the sewer. "But you told us not to bother with Samuel Skipstone," she said.

"Changed my mind," said Dr Skully, brushing aside his greasy ginger hair.

"You won't believe what we found down there, sir!" said Luke as he and Resus clambered out of the tunnel. "There's this massive cavern and—"

He froze. Dr Skully didn't have ginger hair…

Dixon's fist smashed into Luke's face and the world went black.

Chapter Twelve
The Machine

Luke woke to find himself in a cage. He couldn't see much because the bars were covered in a sheet, and listening was proving pointless: all he could hear was the blood pumping through the worst headache he'd ever had.

He searched through his pockets, grunting in frustration. *Skipstone's Tales of Scream Street* and Count Negatov's fang had gone.

"There's a troll playing drums in my skull!" Resus lay beside him, clutching his head. "Where's my cloak?" he asked. "And where's Cleo?"

Luke was about to admit that he didn't know the answer to either question when the sheet was torn away. "You *know* where you are!" boomed a voice. "You've already been here – TO STEAL MY BOOK!"

The cage had been set up in the secret room beneath Sir Otto's library. The landlord was holding *Skipstone's Tales of Scream Street* up to the bars. Dixon lurked behind him, wearing Resus's cape.

"However, as you've brought me a little gift, I'll accept your apology." Sir Otto produced Count Negatov's fang and clamped it under his lip. "Look at me, Dikthon!" he lisped. "I'm a vampire, just like our friend here!"

"Count Negatov will rise up and tear you apart!" roared Resus.

The landlord's face broke into a dark smile. "So, this *is* the fang of Negatov," he snarled. "Thank you for confirming my suspicions. Samuel

Skipstone told me about the relics of the founding fathers. Soon their power will be mine!"

"That's not true," shouted Luke. "Skipstone would never speak to you!"

"That's what I thought too," grinned Sir Otto, "but it would appear that I've been treating his book entirely the wrong way. I was trying to coax information out of Skipstone, when all I had to do was this…"

Opening the book, Sir Otto began to tear slowly at the corner of one of the pages. Samuel Skipstone screamed in agony. "I'm sorry, Luke," he cried. "He forced me to tell him about the relics!"

"I'll kill you," Luke yelled at Sir Otto. "I'll rip your heart out!"

"Which is exactly why I've got you locked in a cage," jeered the landlord.

"Where's Cleo?" demanded Resus.

"Ah, the mummy," sighed Sir Otto dramatically. "She proved to be quite the little fighter!" The landlord snapped his fingers.

Dixon pressed a series of buttons on a wall-mounted console. A section of the floor slid away to reveal a vast machine below. Cleo was strapped to the top of it.

"That's the generator!" cried Resus. "The generator that used to provide Scream Street with its electricity! I've seen pictures of it!"

"Only now its power has been adapted," said Sir Otto. "Instead of creating electricity, it drags the spirits of the dead from below and fuses them with energy!"

"You're – you're making poltergeists," said Resus. "You're not controlling the poltergeists, you're *making* them!"

"Clever, isn't it?" beamed Sir Otto proudly, stroking his silk scarf. "Who would have thought you freaks would be more use to me dead than alive?"

"The dead should be allowed to rest in peace!" shouted Resus.

"Which is why I've decided to experiment with a live specimen," grinned Sir Otto, gesturing towards Cleo. "By my calculations, the first blast of electricity should stop her heart, transferring control of her spirit directly to me."

"I'd like to see you try!" yelled Resus. "Her heart is—"

"My heart is in good condition," interrupted Cleo, throwing Resus a warning look. "Bring it

 123

on, Sneer," she teased. "Do your worst!"

The landlord thrust the fang and *Skipstone's Tales of Scream Street* into his pocket. "Oh, I do like it when they're feisty," he grinned, waddling to the console and adjusting a dial. The generator beneath Cleo started to hum.

"As soon as he flicks the switch, we move," whispered Luke to Resus. The vampire nodded, keeping his eyes fixed on Dixon as he checked the cables.

Sir Otto turned. "Say goodbye to your organs, bandage girl!" he grinned, pulling the lever to turn the generator to full power.

Cleo's whole body jolted as the first blast of electricity roared through her. She barely had time to feel thankful that her heart and other organs were safe in her bedroom before another bolt of power brought with it a second shock.

"Now!" said Luke.

Using his false fingernails, Resus picked the lock on the cage door. As Dixon realized what the vampire was doing, he rushed across the room to stop him, but he was too late.

The door hit Dixon full in the face and he staggered to one side as Luke dashed out. Resus

 124

reached through the bars to grab his cloak. He pulled hard and Dixon's skull hit the cage with a clang.

Stunned by the blow, Dixon's shape-shifting mechanism was forced into overdrive. Resus yanked back again and again, changing Sir Otto's nephew into Tibia Skully, Doug and even Sir Otto himself as he bounced off the cage. Finally, just as the skinny man became Eefa Everwell, Resus tied his hair to the bars.

Sir Otto could hear nothing of the commotion behind him, the rattles and buzzes of the now fully active generator drowning out everything else. He continued to puff on his cigar and watch the dials of the machine.

As another surge of electricity passed through her body, Cleo looked up and saw Luke staring down at her from above. "I'm … fine…" she groaned through gritted teeth. "Get … the … fang!"

It wasn't until Luke was almost upon him that the landlord realized the cage was open. Turning, Sir Otto punched Luke hard in the stomach. "You can't stop me," he shouted. "You and your pathetic parents are trapped here for ever!"

Lashing out, Luke ripped the silk scarf away from the landlord's neck and froze. Sir Otto's throat was missing. Where there should have been skin was simply a tangled mass of flesh and bone, held together by strips of scar tissue.

"I grew up on this filthy street!" screamed Sir Otto. "My parents spent all their time making sure the monsters were happy. Even when I was attacked and *this* happened, the freaks always came first!" He held his cigar in front of Luke's face. "If it wasn't for the magic contained in these, I wouldn't be able to breathe at all!"

The landlord kicked Luke to the ground. "You freaks will pay," he spat. "When I have all the relics, I will banish everyone in this rotten street to the fires of the Underlands for all eternity!"

Luke felt the familiar sensation of change wash over him, but this was no partial transformation. His face stretched outwards, teeth bursting from bloody gums. Claws ripped through the ends of his fingers as hair sprouted from his entire body.

Within seconds, Luke was in his full werewolf form. He leapt to his feet and advanced on Sir Otto, snarling.

 126

The landlord grabbed a wrench from the tool-box at his feet and swung it at Luke, catching him on the shoulder. The wolf howled in pain and leapt forward, clamping its powerful jaws onto Sir Otto's arm and biting hard.

The wrench struck Luke across the face this time, sending him crashing to the floor. The landlord snatched up the entire toolbox and hurled it. The werewolf twisted to one side and the heavy metal box smashed harmlessly beside him.

A scream rang out. "Resus!" cried Cleo. "Something's happening!"

Resus banged Dixon's head against the cage one final time and turned to peer down at Cleo. Smoke was beginning to rise from the mummy's bandages.

"There's something else here," shouted Cleo. "No – some*one*! The machine's pulling another spirit up from the dead!"

Resus raced for the control panel as the generator started to shake violently.

The battle between Luke and Sir Otto continued to rage. The wolf's jaws snapped together again and again as the landlord lashed out with the wrench. Sir Otto lunged at Luke. The wolf

leapt into the air and the landlord crashed into a bank of machinery, becoming entangled in the wiring.

Luke leapt on top of Sir Otto and howled, baring his teeth for the kill. The landlord screamed and closed his eyes as the wolf lunged forward. There was a rip as Luke tore open Sir Otto's pocket, grabbing both *Skipstone's Tales of Scream Street* and Count Negatov's fang with his teeth.

Luke climbed off the landlord and growled. Sir Otto sobbed helplessly. The wolf, content the fight was over, padded over to where Cleo was strapped down.

"Stop the generator, Resus!" bellowed Cleo. "It's coming!"

"I'm trying!" shouted Resus, flicking switch after switch. The vampire could only watch as light began to shine from the gaps between Cleo's bandages.

A roar filled the room. Sir Otto, who had only been pretending to cry, charged at Luke. The wolf flipped onto his back and thrust his legs in the air, pressing them hard into the landlord's stomach.

Kicking with all his might, Luke flipped Sir Otto over his head and down towards the generator below. The landlord crashed on top of the machine, smashing Cleo's restraints and allowing her to wriggle to one side just as a fully formed poltergeist burst out of the generator with a scream.

Resus watched in horror as the bolt of pure energy shot through the air towards Luke. Diving towards his friend, he snatched *Skipstone's Tales of Scream Street* from the wolf's jaws, using the metallic silver cover to deflect the screeching ghost across the room and into the control panel on the wall.

The console exploded. Cables and wires fizzed with energy as the poltergeist was fed back into the machine that had created it.

The generator dropped to a low hum, Cleo slumped back against the unconscious landlord and Resus watched in amazement as the single electric light bulb that hung from the ceiling flick-ered into life.

Chapter Thirteen
The Gift

"**This way,**" said Resus to the queue that snaked through his house and down into the cellar. Luke was in the sewer tunnel below, passing up books, paintings and ornaments as the residents of Scream Street came to reclaim what Sir Otto had confiscated from them.

"Any sign of the goblins?" the vampire called down through the trapdoor.

Luke shook his head. "I guess they don't feel safe down here any more."

"Not since you tried to blow them up, anyway," grinned Resus. He glanced over his shoulder as Eefa Everwell arrived. "How's Cleo?"

"She'll be fine," said the witch. "She's in bad shape at the moment, but after a few days' bed rest she'll be running around as normal."

"I hope not," said Resus. "We're getting a bit fed up of having to rescue her every ten minutes, aren't we!" He glanced at Luke to find his friend staring at Eefa, once again lost in her enchantment. He laughed. "You'd better close your mouth in case another rat comes flying past!"

Dr Skully and Alston Negative appeared beside Luke in the tunnel. "That's the last of the items," said the teacher. "Now, if you and Resus would be good enough to show us where this secret room is…"

Dixon opened the gates to Sneer Hall without complaint. "I'm sorry," he whined, rubbing at the bald patches on his head. "Uncle Otto made me do it!"

"Where is he now?" asked Luke.

"In his room," replied Dixon. "He says he won't come out for anyone."

"That'll save us some trouble," said Alston.

Luke led the way to Sir Otto's library and pulled the book out from its position on the shelf. With a click, the secret door opened.

"A basic pulley mechanism," said Dr Skully, examining the bookcase. "Shouldn't be too difficult to disable. This door won't be used again."

Alston followed Luke and Resus down the steps and into the stone room. Clumps of ginger hair were still knotted around the bars of the cage.

"Looks like Dixon had to pull himself free to get to Sir Otto," said Resus.

"He must have been tearing his hair out with worry!" Luke quipped.

Alston checked the settings on the control panel, pressing various buttons to ensure the dials were reading as they should. "It all looks to be in working order," he said. "Blasting that poltergeist back into the machine must have tripped the reset switch and set it running in the right direction again."

"So, Scream Street's going to get its electricity supply back?" asked Resus.

"As long as the wiring is still intact," replied Alston. "I've got someone checking that as we speak."

A handful of stone crumbled from the wall and a green head appeared, a screwdriver clenched between rotten teeth. "Everything looks hunky-dory to me, dudes!" grinned Doug. "Fire her up!"

Alston pulled a lever on the console and the generator rattled into life.

"Uh-oh!" said Doug, sniffing the air. "I think something's burning…"

Luke held his nose. "That's not burning," he said. Snatching up the sheet that had covered the cage, he found Squiffer crouched there, hiding behind his hands. Luke grabbed him, causing the terrified goblin to let off another blast of noxious gas.

"You be leave me alone!" Squiffer screeched. "Or I be go and tell flabby man about you!"

"I think you've told Sir Otto enough," said

Luke. "Although I agree that you should probably spend a bit more quality time together!"

Climbing the stairs, Resus followed the stench of cigars to Sir Otto's bedroom. He opened the door to discover the landlord lying on his bed, an ice pack on his head and face mask over his eyes.

"Is that you, Dixon?" Sir Otto growled without looking up. "I thought I told you that I didn't want to be disturbed!"

Squiffer let loose a silent burst of gas and Luke was forced to cover his mouth, both against the stench and for fear of laughing.

"Well, seeing as you're here now," continued the landlord, "see if you can do something about the drains. Since those impudent young freaks invaded the sewers, the pipes have stunk like a troll's armpit!"

"I've always said it takes one bad smell to know another," said Luke.

Sir Otto ripped the mask from his eyes. "You!"

"We came to see how you're feeling," said Resus. "It can't be nice having a poltergeist pass right through you."

"Maybe that's where they get their famous tempers from?" grinned Luke.

"I'll get you!" roared the landlord, struggling to climb off the bed.

Luke pulled a face. "And to think, we came to bring an old friend for a visit!" He tossed Squiffer into the room and slammed the door. Resus slid a false fingernail into the lock and closed it with a click.

"No!" screamed Sir Otto, rattling the door as an *eep!* escaped from the goblin. "Get me away from this thing. Let me out!"

Resus smiled as wafts of green cloud seeped beneath the door. "Do you think they'll be OK in there?"

Luke nodded. "Trust me," he said. "They'll have a gas!"

Luke sat on the edge of his bed, blasting the evil army of mechanoids that invaded his games console. Since the electricity supply had been restored, the residents of Scream Street had been pulling all kinds of appliances out of retirement. Luke was just happy his games were working again.

He reached the end of the level and pressed

a series of buttons to activate his rocket launcher as the robot overlord hovered into view.

"These moving stories really are very exciting!" exclaimed Samuel Skipstone from the cover of his book on the bedside table. "And I used to think pencil illustrations were advanced!"

There was a knock at the door. "Come in," called Luke, pausing the game.

Mr and Mrs Watson entered the room with a tray of food. Luke didn't need his werewolf sense of smell to identify the dinner: beefburger and chips.

"How are you feeling?" Luke asked his mum, indicating her bandaged arm.

"I'll live," she said.

Luke's dad jumped as a skeletal dog burst into the room and leapt up at him, barking. Cleo and Resus appeared in the doorway. "Scapula wanted to come and say hello," explained the mummy. She was wrapped in fresh white bandages and had applied make-up to those across her face.

Resus had re-dyed his hair jet black and smoothed it all down with gel. His face was once again coated in white face paint and his cloak had a new electric-blue lining.

"We'll leave you to it," said Mr Watson, throwing Resus a nervous glance.

"Your dad's still not sure about me," grinned the vampire as the door closed.

"I guess it's the whole 'creature of the night' image," said Luke. "You do look pretty scary!"

Resus grinned. "I just have to work out how to hide my reflection in mirrors now. That'll *really* spook people!"

Cleo nudged the vampire. "Go on, then," she said. "Give it to him."

"You give it to him!" said Resus.

"Will one of you tell me what's going on?" said Luke.

Resus shrugged and pulled open his cape. Cleo reached inside and produced a small golden casket. "We thought this would be ideal to keep the book and the relic in until we find the others," she smiled.

Luke took the casket and ran his hands over the hieroglyphics carved into the lid. "Wait a minute," he said, "isn't this where you keep—"

"My heart, liver and kidneys – yes!" beamed Cleo. "But they're better off in the fridge now the power's back on."

Luke pulled Count Negatov's fang from the pocket of his jeans and dropped it into the casket. "I don't know what to say."

"Scapula!" shouted Resus.

"No, it definitely wasn't that," said Luke.

"Scapula, put that down!" yelled Resus. Luke turned to see the dog heading for the door, *Skipstone's Tales of Scream Street* in his mouth.

"Oh, dear!" cried Samuel Skipstone. "I do not like this at all!"

"Scapula!" called Luke, Resus and Cleo as they chased the dog down the stairs, through the front door and out into Scream Street.

Luke's quest continues in:

SCREAM STREET

BLOOD OF THE WITCH

Turn the page to read
the first chapter...

Chapter One
The Blood

Blood trickled down the vampire's fangs. A long tongue flicked out and licked the sticky fluid from sharp, glistening teeth. The vampire's mouth twisted into a smile as it savoured the taste. It wanted more.

Lashing out, the vampire used its yellowing talons to tear another hunk of meat from the carcass. Pausing only to drench it in the nearby pool of blood, the creature bit into strips of flesh, veins

and tendons swinging below its salivating jaw. Suddenly a cry rang out.

"Dad! Leave some for everyone else!"

Alston Negative glanced around the dinner table and slowly placed the chicken wing back onto his plate. "Sorry," he mumbled, shamefaced.

Resus Negative, the vampire's son, reached inside his electric-blue-lined cape and produced a knife and fork. Handing them to his father, he added, "And you know you should be using cutlery when we have visitors."

As Alston fumbled with the unfamiliar tools, Resus nudged his friend, Luke Watson. "You don't make that much mess when you eat – and you're a werewolf!"

Luke grinned as he watched the older vampire push the chicken wing off his plate, catapulting potatoes across the black dining-room carpet.

"Being a vampire does have its advantages," joked Alston, leaping from his chair. "When I'm tired of biting necks, I double as a vegetable rack!" He pecked at the carpet and reappeared with a potato stuck to each fang.

"Dad," groaned Resus, embarrassed. "You're not funny!"

Luke roared with laughter and turned to his parents to share the joke. His face fell when he realized that the get-together hadn't worked. His mum and dad were still terrified of their vampire neighbours.

"A toast!" beamed Alston, pulling the potatoes from his teeth and raising a glass of wine. "To the Watsons, and your first week in Scream Street!"

"The Watsons!" echoed Resus, lifting his tumbler of milk. He clinked it against Luke's and drank deeply, his fangs tinkling against the rim of the glass. Instead of drinking his own milk, Luke reached out to take his mum's trembling hand and guide it towards her wine.

Mrs Watson forced a smile. "Thank you," she whispered hoarsely.

Luke and Resus shared a glance. Luke's family had been moved to Scream Street by G.H.O.U.L., Government Housing Of Unusual Life-forms, after he had transformed into his werewolf form and attacked a school bully. Since then his parents had lived in a state of sheer terror.

In order to open a doorway back to his own world, Luke had begun to search for six relics left behind by the community's founding fathers. The first of these, a vampire's fang, was now locked away in a golden casket under his bed.

"Now," said Bella Negative as she entered carrying a jug of thick red liquid, "who wants more blood on their meat?"

Mr Watson stared at the jug and paled. "I think I'm going to be sick…"

"I'll get you some water," said Luke, racing to the kitchen. Reaching for the cold tap, he stopped. The sink had three taps. "Resus!" he called.

The young vampire hurried in. "You summoned me?" he teased.

"Which one is cold water?" Luke asked.

"Isn't it obvious?" replied Resus. He gestured from left to right. "Hot water, cold water, blood."

"Blood?" exclaimed Luke. "You've got a tap for *blood*?"

"Of course," said Resus. "How else do you think vampires get their fix? We need a regular supply." He spun the tap, allowing a torrent of crimson blood to flow out into the sink. It spattered against the stainless steel, leaving behind small clots and scabs as it raced for the plughole.

"B-but a *tap*?" stammered Luke. "Where does it come from?"

"Whenever anyone has a nosebleed or a cut finger and they rinse the blood away, it ends up in the sewer system," explained Resus. "The blood is filtered out and fed to vampires around the world."

"That's disgusting!"

"No more disgusting than the way our ancestors used to get it." Resus opened his mouth and bared his fangs at Luke with a hiss.

Bella Negative appeared behind him. "Getting a drink of blood?" she asked, ruffling her son's hair.

"Luke knows I'm a normal like his mum and dad," Resus sighed. "He knows I'm not a real vampire!" He unclipped his false fangs and rinsed them briefly under the water before reattaching them to his teeth. Suddenly the stream of blood stopped, the last remaining drips pattering against the sink.

"That's odd," said Resus. He opened the cupboard under the sink and reached past boxes of coffin polish and fang-whitener to check the stopcock.

Luke crouched down beside him. "Maybe there's a safety drive on and people have stopped grazing their knees," he grinned.

"I hope not," said Resus. "My dad gets really cranky without his daily pint!"

"Er, Luke," called Alston from the dining room, "I think your parents are ready to go home now."

Luke stood and turned to see his mum smiling bravely, his dad's arm tight around her shoulders. "I've got to take them away from here," he said quietly to Resus. "They're never going to be happy as long as we're in Scream Street."

"You mean...?" began the young vampire.

Luke nodded. "It's time to find the second relic."

Scream Street has been invaded – by vampire rats...

Luke, Resus and Cleo are already on the trail of the second relic, a vial of witch's blood. But obstacles abound – first the evil Sir Otto Sneer turned off the blood supply, then a swarm of vampire rodents escaped and now all the residents have been infected with vampire Energy! It looks like Luke and his friends will have to choose between finding the relic and saving their neighbours...

SCREAM STREET
Where blood is tastier than water!

Scream Street just got darker...

Scream Street has been shrouded in constant night for as long as anyone can remember, but things look really black when millions of spiders escape from No. 5, covering everything with their suffocating webs. Luke, Resus and Cleo have their work cut out trying to combat the creepy-crawlies while searching for the third relic, the heart of the ancient mummy – and Sir Otto is determined to fight them every step of the way.

SCREAM STREET
It's no place like home!

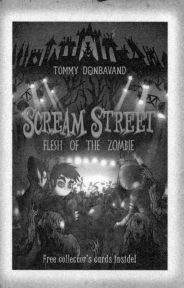

TOMMY DONBAVAND

SCREAM STREET
FLESH OF THE ZOMBIE

Free collector's cards inside!

The zombies have arrived in Scream Street...

Deadstock, the world's greatest zombie rock festival, is here! Sir Otto Sneer, however, is not in the mood for dancing – and causes a riot by banishing headlining flesh-metal band Brain Drain to the evil Underlands. If Luke and his friends want to restore peace to the neighbourhood and find the relic they seek, they'll have to follow the band … into the darkest depths of the earth.

SCREAM STREET
Dead pleased you dropped by!

Tommy Donbavand was born and brought up in Liverpool and has worked at numerous careers that have included clown, actor, theatre producer, children's entertainer, drama teacher, storyteller and writer. His non-fiction books for children and their parents, *Boredom Busters* and *Quick Fixes for Bored Kids*, have helped him to become a regular guest on radio stations around the UK and he also writes for a number of magazines, including *Creative Steps* and Scholastic's *Junior Education*.

Tommy sees his new comedy-horror series as what might have resulted had Stephen King been the author of *Scooby Doo*. "Writing *Scream Street* is fangtastic fun," he says. "I just have to be careful not to scare myself too much!" Tommy lives in Northumberland with his family and sees sleep as a waste of good writing time.

You can find out more about Tommy and his books at his website: www.tommydonbavand.com